Moo Kitty
™
Finds a Home

ISBN: 978-1-60800-010-4
Library of Congress Control Number: 2011932184

Original concept art by Valerie Lee Veltre
Digital illustrations by Liz Leonard

Design and layout by Pamela Haines
Squidgy Press
Lancaster, PA
717 239 0490
Squidgy Press is an imprint of LifeReloaded
www.lifereloaded.com

1 2 3 4 5 W 13 12 11

Designed, published and printed in the
United States of America

Moo Kitty™
Finds a Home

by

Valerie Lee Veltre

squidgy press
Fun for Kids
a smile for
everyone else

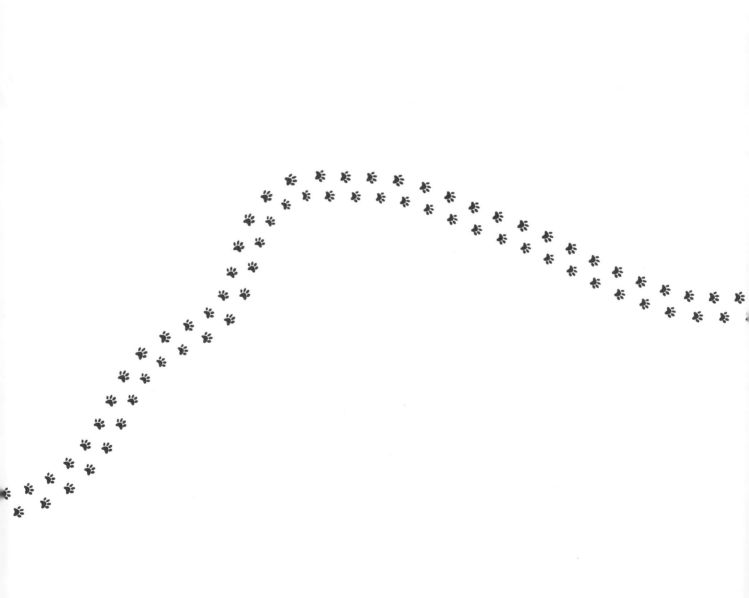

To my Mother & Herb with endless love and gratitude.

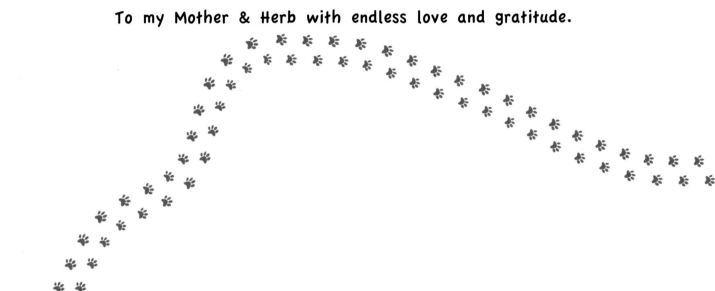

Once upon a time, there lived a black and white spotted cat. His name was Moo Kitty, because he looked like a cow.

He had beautiful green eyes and
was very handsome.

1

Moo Kitty lived with his human.
He loved her very, very much,
and she loved him just
as much.

They lived on a tree-lined street, in a little brick house surrounded by flower gardens and rose bushes.

They spent their days outside in
the garden enjoying the flowers.

Sometimes, Moo would chase butterflies, but most of the time he would doze on the patio in the warmth of the sun.

In the evenings, Moo and his human would sit quietly, she reading a book, while Moo settled in for a pleasant night snuggled in his very own blue blanket.

They were very happy together, and many years passed in each other's treasured company. They were best friends and understood each other completely.

Then came the day Moo Kitty's human went to
heaven. Moo was very sad. He thought they would
always be together.

People came and packed everything up.

Gone was his favorite chair and his warm blue blanket.

He sat in the corner while all he had known was taken away.

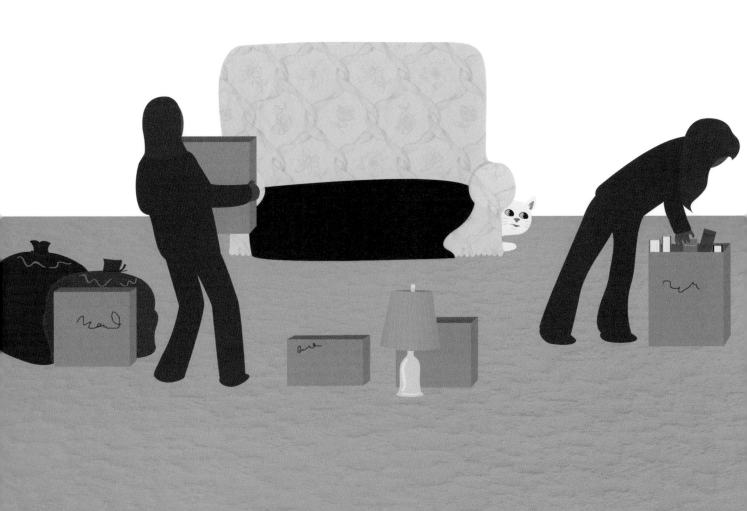

Then he was carried out the door and placed next to the trash cans.

The people left without a backwards glance. He did not understand.

"Wait! Wait!" he cried. "Please! I don't know where to go. I don't know what to do."

He ran to the front door; he ran to the back door. He raced through the garden. He was alone.

Exhausted, he finally lay down under the hostas and cried himself to sleep.

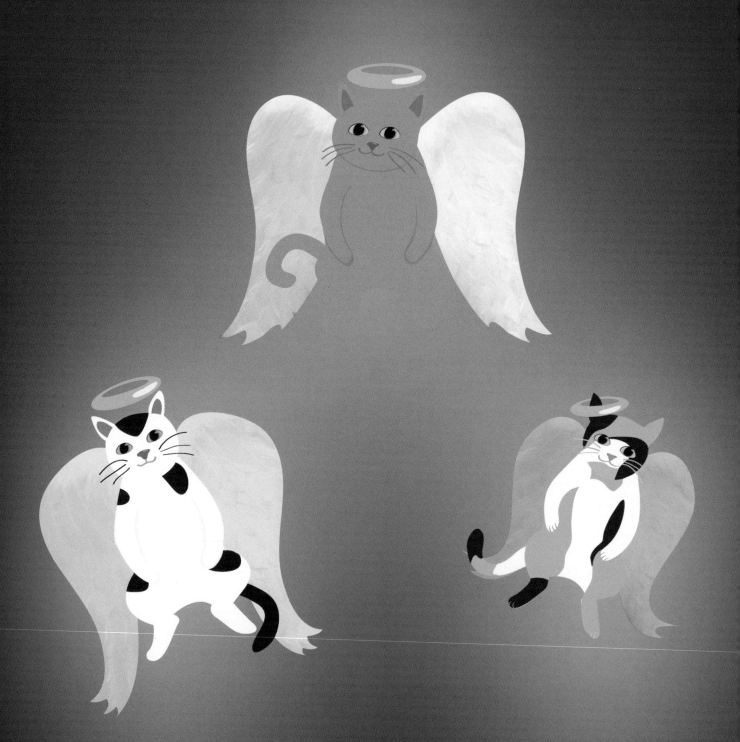

When it was dark, Moo woke up. He was cold and hungry, and he missed his human. He was scared of the darkness and the unfamiliar sounds of the night. He shut his eyes tight.

"Moo Kitty! Moo Kitty! Wake up dear, sweet Moo Kitty," whispered a gentle voice.

Moo opened his eyes. "Oh! Who are you?" he gasped. Three beautiful, shining figures stood before him.

"Don't be afraid; we are here to watch over you," said another kind voice.

"We will help you," said the third.

"We are here to help you, but you will not see us after tonight. Trust that we are always with you, and that you are loved," said Fred.

"But what should I do? How will I know you are with me?"

"You only need to believe and have faith that you are not alone," said Calvin.

"Now sleep, little cat, for tomorrow is a new day."

Moo felt warm and safe. He closed his eyes and dreamed of happy days chasing butterflies and nights snuggled in his blue blanket, lying close to his dear human.

In the morning, Moo woke to the birds chirping, "Good morning Moo! Get up! Get up! Get up sleepyhead! Get up! Get up! Get up out of bed!"

Moo looked around for his new friends, but did not see them. He remembered that they had told him to have faith, and that they would always be with him.

He had to be brave. He had to believe.

He was hungry and knew he'd have to search for breakfast. He looked at his garden for the last time and made his way into the big, unknown world.

Moo walked for a long time.

His paws began to hurt and, his stomach was rumbling. He passed many people, but no one seemed to notice him. He sat down to rest and let out a big sigh.

He thought of his special friends and hoped they were with him.

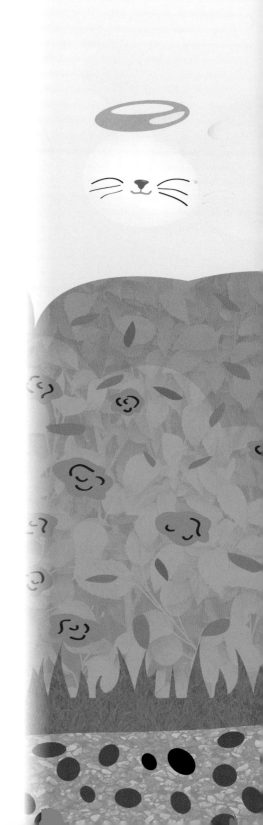

"Well, hello there little kitty! I almost didn't see you."

Moo looked up at a human smiling down at him.

"Are you lost? Are you hungry?"

"Yes I am! Yes I am!"

"Come along now, and we'll get you something to eat."

Moo Kitty followed the nice human to a house. The human knocked on the door.

"Hello, Dolores. I have another stray for you."

"Oh George, I'm so sorry, but I can't possibly take one more. You'll have to take him to the shelter."

"Me, I w... ended u... here. Y... hungry, ... happens ... to you...

"Hey ev...

Moo awoke the next morning to the sound of kittens laughing and playing.

He looked around and realized the room was lined with cubbies full of adult cats and kittens.

There were lots and lots of adorable kittens.

A grey t

Stripes.

"Yes, I j

Moo Kit

"How'd y

street

"My hur

nowher

Many humans came to the shelter.

He would try to look as cute and friendly as he could, but he was always passed over.

He soon learned that the kittens were almost always the first to find new homes.

One by one, the kittens were adopted.

"Good bye Moo!"

"Good bye! Good luck! Don't worry you'll get adopted."

As the weeks went by, Moo began to lose hope. He was afraid he'd never find a new human.

He was happy to be safe at the shelter and happy for the other cats and dogs that were adopted, but he longed for a new home.

One day, his best friend Stripes
was adopted.

"Good bye Moo!" Stripes happily shouted.

"Don't worry. It will be your turn next."

Moo sighed. He realized he was the last one left from his original group of cats and kittens. Even a rabbit had found a home before him.

Time passed, and each day seemed to be the same as the last.

Moo was so sad he hardly paid attention to the humans who came to visit. He thought no one wanted an old cat.

When he felt he was ready to give up hope, he would remember the angel cats and what they had said, and he would hold onto the little flicker of faith deep inside.

It was all he had.

Then one day...

Moo was daydreaming about
dozing on his patio in the warmth
of the sun.

He was suddenly startled by a
young, clear, human voice.

"Look! He looks like a Moo Cow.
He's a Moo Kitty."

Moo sat up. "She knows my name!
She knows my name!"

"Look at his neat eyes. They are
a beautiful shade of green," said
her mother.

"What a handsome cat," said
her father.

The little girl held him, and he pressed himself into her as hard as he could and purred with all his might.

"He's the one! He's the one I want."

"Goodbye George! Goodbye everyone! Don't lose faith. It will happen for you all.

"Just believe, and don't give up hope!"

Moo's new family took him home.

His new house was white with green shutters. It was surrounded by flower gardens and rose bushes. He thought it was perfect.

He was happy. He was home.

So Moo snuggled into his new, soft, mint green blanket and drifted off to sleep, dreaming of roses and butterflies and the happy days to come.

About the Author

Fond of creatures great and small, Valerie believes each deserves love, care, and admiration.

Valerie was inspired to write and illustrate Moo Kitty Finds a Home after she rescued Moo Kitty and gave him a forever home.

Valerie lives on Bee Tree Farm in the heart of Kentucky's bluegrass horse country. She shares her home with a variety of four-legged creatures.

She is an equestrian, enjoys gardening, the outdoors in general, and having a good laugh with friends and family.

Moo Kitty is alive and well. He enjoys inspecting his flower garden and can often be found in his favorite chair, napping on his mint green blanket. Visit valerieleeveltre.com to learn more about Valerie.

About the Illustrator

Liz Leonard is a freelance illustrator who works through a combination of traditional and digital media. She has a BFA in Illustration from the Pennsylvania College of Art & Design. Her interests include children's books, advertising, greeting cards, spot illustration, and textiles.

When not working on art, she likes to read, make crafty things, and be sat on by her cat, Tandy. If interested in seeing more of her work, or if you just want to say hi, you can visit lizleonardillustration.com

Benefits of Adopting an Adult Pet

Moo Kitty is a real cat whose story is based on his real-life experiences. He wants you to understand the benefits you, too, can reap from adopting an adult animal. He also wants to share some tips to make it easier for you, your family (human and animal members), and your new adult pet to adjust, once you bring him or her home.

If you are considering adopting a new pet, don't automatically decide to buy from a breeder or pet store. Consider adopting from a local shelter. Some of the unique advantages of adopting adult animals are:

- You'll reduce the population of strays on the street by opening shelter space for another animal.

- You're saving an adult animal from a potentially hopeless situation. Unfortunately, many are euthanized unless they are in a no-kill shelter.

- The cost of adopting a pet at an animal shelter is far less expensive than buying one from a breeder or pet store.

- Often animals adopted from shelters have already been neutered, wormed and vaccinated.

- You won't have to go through the demanding stages of training a new kitten or puppy because it is likely that the animal:

  - Will be litter/house trained.

  - Will not engage in destructive behaviors common to young, teething animals.

- An adult animal is likely to be socialized to behave well around people and other animals.

- Adult animals are more sedate, making them a practical choice for the elderly and families with children.

- When necessary, an adult animal can be left alone for longer periods of time than a kitten or puppy.

More Benefits

- What you see is what you get:
    - You know pretty well what you're getting with a grown cat or dog, regarding energy/activity level, temperament, sociability and health.
    - An adult animal's personality is pretty much set, giving you a better handle on how well s/he will fit into your household and whether or not s/he'll get along with any other pets.
- Given time in a loving environment, a grown cat forms just as tight a bond with his new human and animal family as any kitten can.
- They know that you have saved them, and constantly show their gratitude.

Of course, every animal is unique and you should expect some differences from one to another. But overall, adopting an adult pet can be—and usually is—a far easier and less disruptive experience than buying a puppy or kitten. And your return on investment in terms of love and gratitude will never be greater.

Adult Animals Make
Great Pets!

Tips For Adopting an Adult Pet

Preparing For A New Pet

- Take your time to search for the right animal for you and your human and animal family members.

- Choose one that fits your household and family lifestyle—e.g. it can be very cramped with a large active animal in a small space.

- Involve all family members in the selection process. Allow and encourage input from everyone, and consider all comments and concerns seriously. Everyone should be happy with the final choice.

Selection

- Understand that even an older pet will require some commitment of time and energy. Do your homework about the needs of certain breeds, and be honest with yourself about what you do—and don't—have to offer.

- Learn what you can about the animal's background, and look for clues to any possible health problems.

- Ask for the animal's health records.

- If possible, have your family vet examine the animal before committing to the adoption.

- Go over the animal from nose to tail. Skin should be clean, supple and unbroken. Most dogs and cats should be covered thickly with a glossy coat of fur. Ears should be clean as well. Eyes should be bright and, like the nose, clear of any discharge. Check the mouth for rosy-pink gums, white teeth, and a lack of disturbingly foul breath, which can be an indicator of many other health issues.

- Spend time playing with the potential adoptee in a quiet area.

- Observe the animal's behavior when he interacts with a variety of people, especially children and men. Fearful behavior can often signal past abuse, and any aggression shown toward children probably indicates a poor choice for a growing family with kids.

- The "right" cat should respond to your attention, relaxing in your lap, pushing for strokes and purring.

- The "right" dog should show similar pleasure in being stroked, and should be content—a wagging tail is always a good sign.

Settling In

- Your new pet will need to learn the rules of your household, but be patient; remember that your adult pet needs time to transition from her former life.

- First impressions are extremely important and leave an indelible imprint on your new pet's psyche.

- Try not to do too much at once. Bring your new pet into the house and let him or her walk around and sniff everything. Don't force the animal toward anything, and if s/he goes where s/he shouldn't, quietly but firmly say, "No," and guide him or her away from that place.

- After your initial walk-through, take the time to show the animal where to take care of bodily functions, where it's okay to lie down and what's "out of bounds."

- Have a few toys ready and make a big show of giving them to your new dog or cat. Having a sense of individual ownership of a few objects will be comforting and make your new pet feel at home.

- Spend quality time petting your new pal, talking with him or her to establish comfort with your voice.

- If your adult pet has trouble seeing or hearing, begin introducing hand signals or touch signals instead of verbal commands.

For more information, visit
MooKittyFindsAHome.com

Moo Kitty™